Bennie Bear's Dream

By
Rachel LaMar

Illustrated by
Emma Kaufmann

BEARS

AuthorHouse™
1663 Liberty Drive
Bloomington, IN 47403
www.authorhouse.com
Phone: 1 (800) 839-8640

Published by AuthorHouse 04/04/2019

ISBN: 978-1-7283-0669-8 (hc)
ISBN: 978-1-7283-0626-1 (sc)
ISBN: 978-1-7283-0625-4 (e)

Library of Congress Control Number: 2019903699

authorHOUSE®

Bennie Bear's Dream

By

Rachel LaMar

Illustrated by

Emma Kaufmann

Dedication

For Zachary and Jenna with all my love.

Bennie Bear had lived in the bear factory for a long time.

He sat at the top of a box of brown stuffed bears, in the very back corner of the factory.

Every day he watched the factory workers come in the morning and sit at their sewing machines. By the end of the day there were more bears piled in boxes by the big doors.

Every Friday the big factory doors would open, and a long truck would back up to the doors.

Men would get out and load boxes of new teddy bears into the back of the truck, and then drive away.

Bennie waited hopefully every Friday.

He just knew that one day it would be his turn to go in the big truck and be driven away to a toy store, and that a wonderful little boy or girl would see him on the shelf and take him home.

This was Bennie's dream-to have a real home and, more importantly, a real child to love him.

One Friday the truck did not come. At the end of the day all the workers went home. Days went by and no one came back to work.

As they waited in the dark factory Bennie heard the other bears talking about what might have happened, but he didn't want to listen to their sad stories.

Bennie wanted to believe that his dream would still come true.

On Wednesday morning the big doors swung open, and a group of men and women in construction hats stood looking into the factory.

They had papers in their hands and they all talked at the same time.

A man stepped into the factory and said "All the machinery will be picked up tomorrow. The wrecking ball will be here next week. There is nothing else we need here. Close it up."

A lady from the group stepped further into the cold factory and looked back into the corner, where there were several boxes of bears.

"What about the teddy bears? There are so many," said the lady, looking up at the stacked boxes. "We can't just leave them here." Bennie saw that she had on a red scarf and wore a friendly smile.

"They can stay," said the man. "We don't have the time to figure out what to do with all those stuffed toys. Just leave them."

The group of people turned to leave.

Bennie knew he had to do something, or his dream would never come true. He pushed with all his might, and the box toppled to the ground. Bennie fell onto the floor.

The lady with the red scarf turned around and walked over to Bennie. She picked him up and looked at his big brown bear eyes and felt his soft fur. She smiled at Bennie.

"I think you are trying to get my attention, aren't you?" she said to Bennie as she patted his head.

The lady with the red scarf bent over and picked up the box of spilled bears and placed the other bears back into it, with Bennie right on top. "You watch the others," she said to Bennie. "I will be back. I have an idea."

Bennie was so excited that he couldn't sleep all night. He knew that something wonderful was going to happen...he could just tell.

The next morning, the big factory doors were opened for the last time. A truck was parked outside, and the lady with the red scarf walked in and pointed to the boxes.

"There they are. Make sure to take every last one of them. I will meet you there."

She handed the truck driver a piece of paper and then left.

The men loaded all the boxes into the truck, closed the doors and drove away.

It was a very long drive, but Bennie didn't mind.

Finally, the truck stopped.

The doors were opened and Bennie tried to peek out over the top of his box. He saw a big building. There was a sign on the building that read "Children's Foster Services."

The men carried the boxes full of bears to the front doors of the building and when the doors opened, out came the lady with the red scarf with a big smile on her face.

She told the men where to put the boxes. Bennie still did not understand what was happening, but he knew it must be something good.

A while later Bennie heard voices-lots of them.

They were the voices of children!

Bennie must have fallen asleep, and he tried to pick himself up to see what was going on, but just then the lady with the red scarf picked him up out of the box.

She held him up for the room full of children to see him.

Next, the lady told all the children that they were to each get their very own bear to love and care for.

Bennie looked at all the happy, smiling faces.

The lady with the scarf called a little girl named Julie up to the front of the room.

She handed Bennie to Julie and told her to take very good care of the bear.

"You mean he is all mine?" said Julie. "I've never had such a perfect stuffed bear!"

Julie put her arms around Bennie and gently hugged him.

"I will take such good care of you," she said. "I love you!"

Bennie looked at Julie and knew that his dream had come true.

Please Help Children Find Forever Homes

There are millions of children looking for their "forever" homes.

Please consider a donation to your local adoption or foster care organizations. For more information on adoption and foster care organizations in your area, please visit your local county adoption department, or search the web for foster care organizations.

A portion of the proceeds from the sale of this book help support foster care organizations and adoption programs.

For speaking engagements, readings, all media, contact
Rachel LaMar / RachelLaMar.com / info@rachellamar.com

CPSIA information can be obtained
at www.ICGtesting.com
Printed in the USA
BVHW020607170419
545711BV00003B/22/P